Moonfall

Moonfall

Farrar, Straus and Giroux

New York

SUSAN WHITCHER

Pictures by BARBARA LEHMAN

To Miss Margaret Sydnor, librarian,
Stoneleigh School, Baltimore
—S.W.

To Mr. Maher
—B.L.

Text copyright © 1993 by Susan Whitcher
Illustrations copyright © 1993 by Barbara Lehman
All rights reserved
Library of Congress catalog card number: 92-54643
Published simultaneously in Canada
by HarperCollins*CanadaLtd*
Printed and bound in the United States of America
by Worzalla Publishing Co.
Designed by Martha Rago
First edition, 1993

One night in April, when lilacs bloomed
along the fence and the moon hung like
an earring on the rim of the sky, a terrible thing
happened. Sylvie saw it.

She went tiptoe down the hall to her parents'
bedroom.

"Mommy," she whispered, "the moon is too
low."

Her mother said, "The moon looks low, because
it is passing behind the shoulder of the world.
But really it is up high far away in the cold sky.
Go back to bed."

But Sylvie went to her window.

Soon she came padding back down the hall to her parents' bedroom.

"Daddy," she whispered, "the moon is too near. It's catching in the branches of the lilacs."

Her father said, "The moon looks near, but really it is your eyes that cannot tell if things are large and far away, or if they're small and close. The lilacs are in Mrs. Schwartz's garden. But the moon is up high far away in the night sky.
Now go back to bed."

But Sylvie went to her window.

Soon she came racing back down the hall to her parents' bedroom.

"Mommy! Daddy! The moon fell into the lilac bushes behind Mrs. Schwartz's fence!"

Her parents did not answer. They were asleep.

Then for fifteen nights there was no moon at all.

On the afternoon of the sixteenth day,
Mrs. Schwartz leaned a ladder against her fence to
pick the brown heads off the lilacs.

"What is that trash underneath my bushes?" she
said. "Sylvie, see if you can crawl under, get it out
for me."

The moon was worn down to a crust. Sylvie took it and shook off the ants. She buffed it with the hem of her shirt until she could see the color.

Mrs. Schwartz said, "Sylvie, honey, I don't think that's something you should be playing with. See how the edge is jagged."

"This is the moon, Mrs. Schwartz. It belongs back in the sky."

"But it's all bent up," said Mrs. Schwartz.

"I can straighten it," said Sylvie.

"It's rusty," said Mrs. Schwartz.

"I can polish it," said Sylvie.

Mrs. Schwartz said, "Sylvie, honey, put it in the trash. It's all stained with earth. It can't rise anymore."

"I can wash it," said Sylvie.

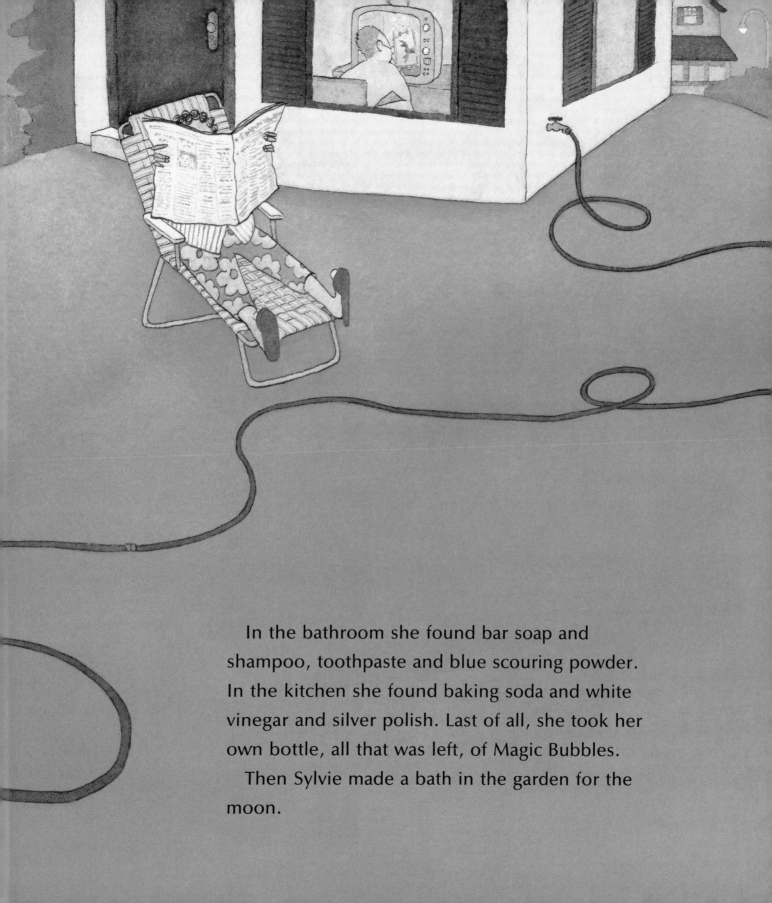

In the bathroom she found bar soap and
shampoo, toothpaste and blue scouring powder.
In the kitchen she found baking soda and white
vinegar and silver polish. Last of all, she took her
own bottle, all that was left, of Magic Bubbles.

Then Sylvie made a bath in the garden for the
moon.

She slipped the moon into the water. The suds
turned gray, then gold, then pale again, and
pearly.

When Sylvie was sure the moon was shining
bright, she felt around under the suds for it.

But the moon was gone.

The moon had melted away. There was nothing
left at the bottom of the tub but the plastic wand
from the Magic Bubble bottle.
  So Sylvie blew a little bubble, a little magic
bubble like a pearl
            like a balloon
                  just like THE MOON.

The bubble rose above the fence and the lilacs.

It rose above the houses and the telephone wires.

It never stopped rising until it was up high,
far away, in the night sky.